Jack Frost's Ice Castle
The Diamond Mountains
Fruit Orchard
Olive Tree
Refreshment Tent
Herb Patch
Refreshments
Insect Habitat
Peace Garden

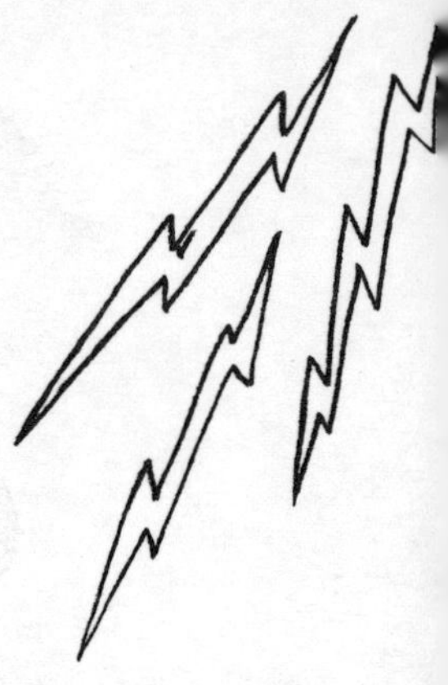

Jack Frost's Spell

I dream of how the world would be
Without respect and harmony:
A land where fairies fuss and fight;
A place that fills me with delight!

I'll steal Jacinda's magic peace,
And see what strife I can release.
No patience, love or kind support.
What fun I'm going to have – what sport!

Jacinda the Peace Fairy

By Daisy Meadows

ORCHARD

www.rainbowmagicbooks.co.uk

Fairyland Palace
Seeing Pool
High Street
Rachel's House
TIPPINGTON TOWN

Contents

Chapter One
Opening Day

"What's the weather like?" asked Rachel Walker, bouncing out of bed and darting to the window. "Oh, I hope it's sunny."

She flung open her curtains and smiled. Sunlight streamed into the room and her best friend, Kirsty Tate, sat up in bed.

"Your wish is granted," she said,

laughing. "I wonder if the Weather Fairies know that today is special."

Rachel and Kirsty had a wonderful secret. They had learned that fairy magic helped the human world every day, even though most people never knew it. Even better, they had made friends with the fairies and shared some exciting adventures with them.

"I don't suppose we'll see any magic today," said Rachel. "It's all about ordinary hard work and people caring for each other."

Rachel's mother had been working on a special project. There was a patch of land in the middle of Tippington town that had been empty for as long as anyone could remember. For years, people had argued about how to use it.

There had been many ideas and lots of squabbling. But at last, everyone had agreed on the perfect answer: a peace garden. After months of hard work, the opening ceremony was today.

"It's such a cool project," said Kirsty as she made her bed. "Were there lots of volunteers?"

"Dozens," said Rachel. "Everyone in

the community wanted to be part of it, and it was Mum's job to organise them all. She's been working really hard."

"Let's go down there straight after breakfast," said Kirsty. "I can't wait to see the garden."

Mr Walker made a yummy breakfast and then the girls walked down to the peace garden. Mrs Walker was already there, and she waved when she saw them.

"I'm glad you're here," she said. "Could you pour some orange juice ready for when the visitors arrive?"

"We'd love to help," said Kirsty.

The girls went over to the refreshment tent. As they were pouring the drinks, Rachel pointed out the people who worked in the peace garden.

"That blonde lady is Marnie, the head gardener," she said. "She's going to make sure that the plants stay healthy, and keep everything looking beautiful and relaxing."

"Who's the red-headed man she's talking to?" Kirsty asked.

"That's Ned," said Rachel. "He is going to run courses in the peace garden to help people relax. He calls it nature therapy. There will be a herb patch, a fruit orchard and lots of insect habitats."

A grey-haired lady in a tweed suit

joined Marnie and Ned.

"That's Erica," said Rachel. "She's in charge of the whole peace garden project."

"Oh, I've run out of juice," said Kirsty. She went to open some more, and gasped.

"Rachel, these cartons are glowing," she whispered. "I think we might see some magic today after all."

The girls leaned closer, and the glow grew stronger. Then a tiny, glittering fairy peeped around the corner of a carton. She was wearing a simple jumpsuit and ballet pumps, and there was a garland of flowers in her dark hair.

"Oh my goodness," Rachel whispered. "Hello, what's your name? Welcome to the peace garden."

"Thank you," said the fairy. "I'm Jacinda the Peace Fairy, and my special magic inspires people to do the right thing and help others. I keep the peace here and in Fairyland."

"It's lovely to meet you," said Kirsty. "Have you come to watch the opening ceremony?"

"Yes," said Jacinda, smiling. "I want to give a little magic to the garden, to make sure it is always a calm and healing place."

"What a lovely idea," said Rachel.

Jacinda took a delicate magnifying glass out of her pocket. It had a rim of pure gold, and the handle was encrusted with sparkling gems.

"This is my magnificent magnifying glass," she said. "It makes sure that people see things from each other's point of view. I'm going to use it to cast a spell over the whole garden, so that it will always be a place of peace."

She held up the glass and the sun beamed through the lens, shining its light across the garden. Jacinda began her spell.

"With this beam of peaceful light
None shall argue, shout or fight.
See the other – oh!"

The magnifying glass was whipped out of her hand. Behind her, a tall figure in a hooded cloak cackled with laughter.

"You're no match for me," he sneered.

He flung back his hood and Jacinda gasped. It was Jack Frost.

Chapter Two
Bad-Tempered Bertram

Jacinda was too scared to speak, but Rachel and Kirsty stepped forward.

"You can't take things that belong to other people," said Kirsty.

"Just watch me," Jack Frost retorted.

He opened his bony hand and showed the girls a cube of solid ice.

The magnificent magnifying glass was trapped inside.

"Oh no!" cried Jacinda.

"Give it back," said Rachel.

"You can't make me," said Jack Frost. "As long as I have this stupid thing, there will be no peace in this world or in Fairyland. Everyone will be lost in a fog of arguments, anger and bad temper, and I can't wait. First stop, the Fairyland Palace. I want to see the queen yelling at the king!"

A sudden blast of icy air whooshed through the refreshment tent, and Jack Frost vanished with a loud *CRACK*.

"This is the worst thing that has ever happened to me," said Jacinda, sinking down on the drinks table with a groan. "Without the magnificent magnifying glass, no one will be able to see another person's point of view. I don't know what to do, and I'm scared of Jack Frost."

"Let us help," said Kirsty at once. "We've faced Jack Frost before. He doesn't seem so scary when you've got friends with you."

Jacinda managed a little smile.

"What should I do now?" she asked.

At that moment, the girls realised that there was a lot of yelling coming from the peace garden. They peeped out of the refreshment tent and saw Marnie and Ned arguing. They were red in the face.

"You can't use this spot for your stupid nature therapy course," Marnie snapped. "I'm still planting here."

"Tough luck," said Ned. "I'll do what I like."

"Hey, I'm in charge around here," said Erica, stepping between them. "Shut up and listen to me."

Jacinda shook her head.

"This is all because the magnifying glass is in the wrong hands," she said.

"Let's try to calm everyone down," said Kirsty.

Rachel felt a rush of anger.

"What a silly idea," she said. "We have to go to the palace and get the magnifying glass back."

"There's no need to be rude," said Kirsty, folding her arms. "You're so bossy."

"Only because I have the best ideas," Rachel retorted.

Jacinda pointed her wand at a little olive tree just outside the refreshment tent. Instantly, one of the branches gave a shake and twisted its narrow leaves into three delicate garlands. Two were human sized, and the third was tiny. No one saw

the garlands fly through the air and land on the heads of the girls and Jacinda. As soon as they were in place, Rachel and Kirsty felt their anger melt away.

"I'm sorry," said Rachel. "I don't know why I was so mean."

"I'm sorry too," said Kirsty. "It must

be because Jack Frost has taken the magnifying glass. Thank you for making us sensible again, Jacinda. Did you cast a spell on the olive tree?"

Jacinda smiled. "Olive leaves are symbols of peace," she said. "With the help of a little fairy dust, they can protect you against losing your temper. But this magic won't be powerful enough to protect everyone."

"Then let's go and get the magnifying glass back," said Kirsty. "Your idea was best, Rachel. We have to go to the palace."

The angry voices outside the tent grew even louder.

"There's no time to lose," said Rachel.

Jacinda waved her wand, and the whole refreshment tent started spinning like a merry-go-round. A second later, the girls realised that it was they who were spinning. Dizzily, they reached out for each other and held on tight as Jacinda's magic transfromed them into fairies. Their filmy wings fluttered, and a flurry of golden sparkles whirled around them. Then the tent vanished, and they were floating down beside the pink turrets of the Fairyland Palace.

"Oh no," said Kirsty at once.

Bertram, the frog footman, was standing in the doorway of the palace. He was blocking three fairies from going inside.

"You're not coming in," he exclaimed. "You haven't been invited."

"The queen won't mind," said the closest fairy, her voice trembling.

"Don't try to tell me what the queen will say," Bertram snapped. "I know her better than you do."

Rachel and Kirsty landed in front of Bertram. He frowned at them, which felt horrible. Bertram was usually so kind

and friendly.

"Are you going to stop us from going in?" Rachel asked. "We haven't been invited either."

Chapter Three
Palace Problems

"The queen has told me that you are both always invited," Bertram said, stepping aside.

"Please let these fairies in too," said Kirsty. "I'm sure that everyone just wants to stop Jack Frost from causing any more trouble."

"We didn't ask for your help," said one of the fairies, putting her hands on her hips. "Actually, we don't want to go in after all."

They flew away, elbowing each other crossly.

"We have to find Jack Frost and stop this," cried Rachel.

"He's inside the palace," said Bertram. "Is he the reason why everyone is so grumpy?"

Jacinda nodded and tapped Bertram's head with her wand. An olive garland appeared there, and his frown disappeared at once.

"Please come in, all of you," he said. "Jack Frost went to see their majesties in the throne room, and I heard him laughing."

Exchanging a worried look, Rachel and Kirsty zoomed along the corridor towards the throne room. They burst through the door with Jacinda behind them.

"Queen Titania, King Oberon," Rachel said, panting. "Jack Frost has stolen Jacinda's magnificent magnifying glass and everyone is feeling grumpy and unreasonable."

There was a long silence. Queen Titania stared at them coldly from her ornate throne. King Oberon was slumped in his seat, his arms folded across his chest, glowering at the fairies. There was a spluttering sound and then Jack Frost stepped out from behind the thrones, grinning from ear to ear.

"This is the best fun ever," he said, sniggering. "They've been arguing about what colour toothbrushes they have."

He skipped out of the throne room, and the fairies curtsied to the king and queen.

"I've never seen the queen looking so unfriendly," Kirsty whispered.

"The king looks as if he's sulking," Rachel said. "Jacinda, will your olive tree magic work on their majesties?"

"I hope so," said Jacinda.

She waved her wand and a small olive garland appeared on the queen's head. At once, she smiled at the fairies. But there was no garland for the king.

"I can't spread more peace without the magnifying glass," said Jacinda, rather breathless.

"You've done all you can, Jacinda," said

the queen in her usual kind way. "I just hope that with Rachel and Kirsty's help, you will be able to find what is rightfully yours. I will take care of the king until your magnifying glass is returned."

"Yes, Your Majesty," they chorused.

Then they turned and zoomed after Jack Frost. As they went, they passed several footmen and fairies, and every single one of them was scowling or quarrelling. Jack Frost giggled as he capered in and out of the grand rooms.

"Jack Frost is the only one who is calm and happy," said Kirsty.

"That's a sentence I never thought I would hear," Rachel remarked.

Jacinda took a deep breath.

"I have to be brave," she said. "I can't let him spoil everything."

She flew swiftly and landed in front of Jack Frost. Rachel and Kirsty quickly joined her.

"Please return my magnifying glass now," Jacinda said, holding out her hand.

Jack Frost smiled, reached out and shook her hand.

"I regret to say that the answer must be no," he replied.

"You've had your fun," said Kirsty. "Now do the right thing."

"I'm sorry to disagree with you," said Jack Frost. "But I haven't had nearly enough fun yet. I want to see just how much trouble I can cause."

There was a blue flash and a loud thunderclap, and he was gone.

"Did you notice something odd about him?" Kirsty asked.

Before anyone could reply, there was a shout and a smash of crockery from the kitchens. Angry voices began to shout, and Bertram came running down the corridor towards them in a panic.

"Goodness gracious," he exclaimed, flapping his webbed hands. "Everything is topsy-turvy! Higgledy-piggledy! No one is themselves."

"Dear Bertram, please try not to worry," said Rachel, putting her arm around him. "We're going to put everything right, just you wait and see."

She sounded so confident that Kirsty and Jacinda felt better too.

"Where has he gone?" asked Bertram, looking around.

"That's a very good question," said Kirsty. "Do you think that the queen would let us use the Seeing Pool?"

"Use whatever you need," said a voice. "Fairyland is depending on you."

They spun around and saw Queen Titania leading the king out of the throne room. He was muttering crossly.

"Thank you," Kirsty said, curtseying again. "We won't let you down."

Chapter Four
The Dark Forest

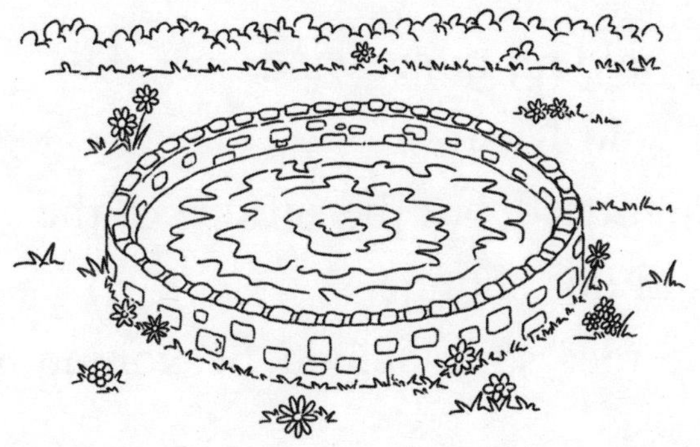

Kirsty led the way through the palace orangery and into the garden, where a little pond sparkled in the sunshine.

"The Seeing Pool," Jacinda whispered in wonder. "I've heard about it, of course, but I've never seen it. What do I have to do to make it work?"

Rachel and Kirsty had been here several times before. They knew that the pool allowed the queen to see what was happening anywhere in Fairyland. But they had never made the magic happen before.

"Try holding your wand over the water," said Kirsty.

Jacinda tried, but the surface of the pond did not change.

"Help me," said Jacinda, beckoning to them.

Gently, Rachel and Kirsty rested their hands on top of hers. Then they all spoke together.

"We want to see Jack Frost."

The water shimmered with golden fairy dust, and then a picture formed. They saw Jack Frost in a dark forest. He was walking towards a white cottage with a red roof, and he was rubbing his hands together.

"Where is he?" asked Jacinda. "I've never seen that place."

"I have," said Kirsty. "Do you

remember, Rachel?"

"Yes, we went there with Robyn, the Christmas Party Fairy," said Rachel. "It's the Barn Elf's house."

"Why is Jack Frost visiting him?" Jacinda asked.

"Why does Jack Frost do anything?" Kirsty replied. "He wants to cause trouble. The Barn Elf is cheeky and loves to play tricks. He once told us that he sometimes helps Jack Frost make mischief."

"I think that we should visit the forest too," said Rachel. "Right now!"

Soon the three fairies were swooping down into the dark green forest where the Barn Elf lived. The last time they were here, plumes of pink smoke and delicious scents had filled the air. Today, the forest seemed very different. There

was a sharp, burning smell among the trees, and no birds were singing.

They reached the cottage and walked around to the back. Just then the door opened and Jack Frost stumbled down the step. Behind him, a small elf with a long white beard was shooing him out with a broom.

"I'm not starting a battle with the fairies just to please you," he shouted. "The Barn Elf doesn't take orders from the likes of you or anyone else."

"Oh thank goodness," said Jacinda. "He's on our side."

"Wait!" Kirsty exclaimed.

But Jacinda had already darted forwards. Rachel and Kirsty shared a worried look. They knew that the Barn Elf wasn't loyal to anyone.

"Thank you for standing up for us," Jacinda said.

The Barn Elf jumped and narrowed his beady eyes.

"What are you doing popping out of nowhere like that?" he growled. "I live in the middle of the dark forest so that I can be alone, not so that fairies and Frostface here can come pestering me."

"But you've refused to help Jack Frost," said Jacinda, clasping her hands together. "Doesn't that mean you're on our side?"

"Not likely," said the Barn Elf. "Scram, the lot of you."

He went back into his cottage and slammed the door. Jack Frost chuckled and bowed to the fairies.

"Bad luck," he said. "The Barn Elf isn't the only magical creature who lives in the forest. I expect there will be a battle soon, with or without his help. Mischief-making, tra-la-la, happy times, tra-la-la."

He cartwheeled around them in a circle. Jacinda looked bewildered, but a tiny idea flickered in the back of Rachel's mind.

"Do you know what I think?" she said loudly. "I think that the magnifying glass is starting to affect Jack Frost. Even though he's working against us, I've never heard him being so polite."

Jack Frost stopped cartwheeling and stared at her. The smile had been wiped off his face.

"That doesn't seem possible, if you don't mind me saying so," he said.

He clapped his hand over his mouth,

and Rachel nodded.

"You see?" she said, turning to her friends.

"I won't allow this," said Jack Frost. "I'm going home. A few minutes with the goblins will get me back to normal."

There was another blue lightning bolt, and he had vanished.

"Luckily, this time we know exactly where he's gone," said Kirsty. "To the Ice Castle!"

Chapter Five
Mountain Mission

Rachel, Kirsty and Jacinda rose into the sky and raced across Fairyland. It was sunny and the rounded hills were bright green. The toadstool houses were as charming as usual. But the land was dotted with groups of fairies arguing. They heard angry voices and slamming doors. Even the birds they passed in the sky were jabbering crossly at each other.

When they reached the frozen land where Jack Frost lived, the first thing they saw was two white foxes rolling in the snow.

"They must be fighting," said Jacinda, slowing down. "Shall we go and separate them?"

"I don't think they're fighting," said Kirsty in a surprised voice. "I think they're playing."

At the Ice Castle, there were more surprises in store. The goblin guards on the battlements were leaning on the icy walls, chatting and laughing. Others were playing board games, and Rachel even spotted two of them practising dance moves.

"What is going on?" Kirsty asked.

"I think I know," said Jacinda, smiling. "My magnificent magnifying glass is working hard, even though it's trapped in

ice. Because Jack Frost has it, the magic is working on him and all his followers. They're calm and tolerant, even though they don't want to be."

Rachel fluttered down to one of the goblin guards.

"Hello," she said. "I would like to see Jack Frost, please."

"I'm sorry, but that won't be possible," said the goblin in a quiet, polite voice. "He doesn't want to have anything to do with the fairies."

"Besides," added another guard, "he's not even here."

"Not here?" Rachel repeated. "But he said that he was coming home."

They were joined by more goblin guards, all nodding eagerly.

"Yes, he was here, but he couldn't stay," said the first goblin. "He said that we were rather quiet and tiresome."

"He wanted things to go back to normal," Rachel said. "It must have been a shock to find his castle filled with harmony and peace."

"That's right," said the second goblin. "He couldn't bear to think that we might become as annoying as you, if you don't mind me saying so."

"Where did he go?" Kirsty asked.

"He said that there is only one way to destroy the magnifying glass," the goblin replied. "He has set off on a noble quest."

"There's nothing noble about that quest," said Jacinda in a worried voice. "I know exactly where he's gone. The only thing that will break my magnifying glass is a rock from the Diamond Mountains. He must be on his way there, and when he arrives he's going to smash the magnifying glass."

Her voice shook, and Rachel squeezed her hand.

"We won't let that happen," she

promised. "Where are the Diamond Mountains?"

"They're even further than the Blue Ice Mountains, where Alyssa the Snow Queen Fairy lives," said Jacinda.

"Then we're going to need something

warm to wear," said Kirsty.

Jacinda flicked her wand, and each of them was wrapped up warm in a snuggly onesie. Then, with another flick, a stream of golden sparkles spiralled from the tip of her wand.

"The fairy dust will guide us," she said. "No matter what happens, keep following the sparkles. I've heard that wild winds and icy storms swirl around the Diamond Mountains."

The goblins waved politely as the fairies set off on their journey. They flew over Goblin Grotto, where all the goblins lived. They flew past the Blue Ice Mountains and over Alyssa the Snow Queen Fairy's tower home. All the time, they kept their eyes on the ribbon of golden fairy dust that rolled out ahead, showing them the way. The wind rose, blowing their hair back and turning their noses and ears pink with cold. Tiny specks of hail peppered them, and a whistling wind shook their wings and made them bump into each other.

"Let's hold hands," cried Kirsty over the noise.

"We're almost there," said Jacinda.

Ahead, mountains as smooth as glass made a spiky skyline. Their peaks glittered with jewels. Halfway up the nearest mountain, a dark figure stood out, its cloak whipping in the wind.

"That's him," cried Rachel, putting on a burst of speed. "That's Jack Frost!"

Chapter Six
Diamond Danger

The fairies landed in a semicircle around Jack Frost. He pressed his back against the mountainside, holding the magnifying glass in its block of ice.

"I am afraid it appears you are too late," he said.

It was strange to hear him using such

polite words. He narrowed his eyes, and his spiky beard shook.

"I very much dislike the way your magnifying glass makes me talk," he went on. "Kindly move aside so that I can smash it to smithereens."

"We won't let you do that," said Kirsty. "The human world and Fairyland need harmony and peace."

"I disagree," said Jack Frost. "I don't want you to have the magic back, but I'm tired of being polite. Also, well-behaved goblins are no fun. So I am going to find the biggest, hardest rock on this mountain and crush the magnifying glass to pieces."

"We won't let you," said Jacinda.

"You don't have any choice," said Jack Frost grumpily.

The fairies exchanged worried looks. He was right. How could they stop him? He was bigger and stronger than they were. He took a step forward and peered over the side of the mountain. Then his knobbly knees knocked together.

"I'm going," he said. But his legs didn't seem to want to obey. Feeling nervous, Rachel reached out her hand and put it on his arm.

"Are you scared of heights?" she asked him kindly.

"Absolutely not," said Jack Frost, gulping loudly. "Er, but how do you climb down, by the way?"

"I don't understand," Kirsty whispered. "Why doesn't he just magic himself down the mountain again?"

"That's one of the strange things about the Diamond Mountains," Jacinda explained. "Magic loses its power up here. That's why this is the place where magical objects can be destroyed."

Rachel still had her hand on Jack Frost's arm. She felt sorry for him because he looked so frightened.

"Please, give back the magnifying glass," she said. "We can get you down from here."

"How?" asked Jacinda. "I can't use magic up here."

"I've had an idea about that," said Rachel.

Jack Frost shook his head.

"I'll never give it back," he declared.

"But you can't move," said Rachel. "You can't destroy it if you can't move."

"Watch me," said the Ice Lord.

He raised the hand carrying the ice block.

"No!" the fairies cried out.

Jack Frost flung the ice block at the mountainside as hard as he could. *SMASH!* Rachel lunged forwards and crouched over the broken lumps of ice. Then she turned, her face beaming. The magnificent magnifying glass was in her hand.

"Yes!" Kirsty cheered.

"How did you do that?" wailed Jack Frost.

With shining eyes, Jacinda took the magnifying glass and slipped it into her

pocket. Rachel turned to Jack Frost.

"We can't use magic to get you down, but we're strong," she said. "We can help to fly you home to the Ice Castle."

"You interfering ninnies!" Jack Frost raged. "You pesky pests! You spoiled everything!"

"Don't you want us to help you?" asked Rachel.

Jack Frost scowled and ground his teeth, but managed a single nod. Rachel and Kirsty hooked their arms under his, and then rose into the air.

"Careful, fools!" he shouted. "Hold on

tight. Don't joggle me. Hurry up!"

He kept up a steady stream of complaints all the way to the Ice Castle. They set him down on the battlements, where the goblin guards were busy squabbling. Jack Frost staggered on wobbly legs, and shook his fist.

"Clear off," he yelled. "No fairies allowed!"

"Things are definitely back to normal," said Kirsty as they flew away. "Thank goodness. I think Jack Frost being polite was the scariest part of the whole adventure."

Rachel and Jacinda laughed, and then Jacinda waved her wand in a large circle. A swirling tunnel of rainbow colours opened up in the air.

"It's time for us to return to the peace garden," she said. "After all, I still have a spell to perform."

One by one, the fairies flew into the tunnel. Rachel and Kirsty rolled out at the other end, human again. Their onesies and olive-leaf gardands had vanished and they were back in the refreshment tent where they had begun their adventure.

"Not a second has passed since we left," said Jacinda, fluttering on to Kirsty's shoulder.

Rachel peeped out of the tent. Marnie and Ned were laughing and smiling together, and Erica was chatting to Mrs Walker. It was as if the earlier arguments had never happened.

"Thank you, Rachel and Kirsty," said the little fairy. "The world can live in harmony again, all thanks to you."

"It was a team effort," said Rachel.

"We enjoyed helping," Kirsty added.

"I owe you a great favour," said Jacinda. "People take peace and understanding for granted until they are lost. Thanks to you, no one has to live without them. Now I have a gift for you and for your town."

She held up the magnificent magnifying glass and let the sunshine stream through. Once again, it lit up the garden with bright light. Jacinda spoke some magic words.

"With this beam of peaceful light,
None shall argue, shout or fight.
See the other point of view,
And in this space you will be true."

For a second the garden shimmered with magical light. The grown-ups who had noticed it blinked and rubbed their eyes. Then they shook their heads. Jacinda smiled.

"Adults never believe in magic, even if they happen to see it," she said.

"Thank you for your wonderful spell," said Rachel. "Now we can be certain that the garden will be a success."

"Of course it will," Jacinda replied. "I hope to visit it often and meet you here again."

She blew them kisses, and then they

heard Mrs Walker calling their names.

"It must be time for the grand opening," said Rachel.

Jacinda disappeared in a twinkle of fairy dust and the girls exchanged a happy smile.

"What an adventure," Rachel said. "I never knew that peace could be so exciting."

"Or that Jack Frost could be so polite," Kirsty agreed, laughing. "I can't wait to find out what our next adventure will be!"

The End

Now it's time for Kirsty and Rachel to help ...

Deena the Diwali Fairy

Read on for a sneak peek ...

It was teatime in late October. Wetherbury village had already settled down for the night. Every house had its lights glowing and its curtains shut. A blustery wind whirled russet leaves along the pavements. Thick, heavy clouds scudded across the sky.

"The clouds are pressed together as if they can't bear to be apart," said Kirsty Tate, her nose pressed up against the sitting-room window.

"Just like us," said her best friend, Rachel Walker.

The girls shared a happy smile. Rachel

had come to stay for the weekend, and they were looking forward to having lots of fun.

"I wonder if we'll see any of our fairy friends," said Kirsty. "Adventures always seem to happen when we're together."

Magic had been a part of their friendship from the beginning. When they first met, they had been plunged into an exciting mission to save the Rainbow Fairies from Jack Frost and his naughty goblins. Ever since, they had helped the fairies many times.

"Someone's coming to your house," said Rachel, pressing her nose against the window too.

A lady in a glittering sari was walking up the path.

"That's our new neighbour, Mrs

Anand," said Kirsty. "She moved in last month."

The doorbell rang, and they heard Mr Tate go to the door.

"Does she have children?" Rachel asked.

"Yes, a boy called Kirin," said Kirsty. "He's in my class at school."

Just then, Mr Tate called them. They found him standing next to Mrs Anand, beaming at them.

"Mrs Anand has come with a very special invitation for you both," he said.

"This week, Kirin and I are celebrating Diwali," said Mrs Anand. "It's the Hindu festival of lights. Today is the main day of the festival, and to celebrate we're having a party. I'm inviting a few of Kirin's classmates and their parents to join us.

Would you like to come?"

"Yes please," said Kirsty.

"That sounds lovely," said Rachel.

"Come over now if you like," said Mrs Anand. "You can help Kirin with the decorating, and he can tell you a bit more about Diwali."

Calling all parents, carers and teachers!
The Rainbow Magic fairies are here to help your child enter the magical world of reading. Whatever reading stage they are at, there's a Rainbow Magic book for everyone! Here is Lydia the Reading Fairy's guide to supporting your child's journey at all levels.

1

Starting Out

Our Rainbow Magic Beginner Readers are perfect for first-time readers who are just beginning to develop reading skills and confidence. Approved by teachers, they contain a full range of educational levelling, as well as lively full-colour illustrations.

2

Developing Readers

Rainbow Magic Early Readers contain longer stories and wider vocabulary for building stamina and growing confidence. These are adaptations of our most popular Rainbow Magic stories, specially developed for younger readers in conjunction with an Early Years reading consultant, with full-colour illustrations.

Going Solo

The Rainbow Magic chapter books – a mixture of series and one-off specials – contain accessible writing to encourage your child to venture into reading independently. These highly collectible and much-loved magical stories inspire a love of reading to last a lifetime.

www.rainbowmagicbooks.co.uk

"Rainbow Magic got my daughter reading chapter books. Great sparkly covers, cute fairies and traditional stories full of magic that she found impossible to put down" – Mother of Edie (6 years)

"Florence LOVES the Rainbow Magic books. She really enjoys reading now" – Mother of Florence (6 years)

Read along the Reading Rainbow!

Well done – you have completed the book!

This book was worth 1 star.

See how far you have climbed on the Reading Rainbow opposite.
The more books you read, the more stars you can colour in
and the closer you will be to becoming a Royal Fairy!

Do you want to print your own Reading Rainbow?

1) Go to the Rainbow Magic website
2) Download and print out the poster
3) Colour in a star for every book you finish and climb the Reading Rainbow
4) For every step up the rainbow, you can download your very own certificate

There's all this and lots more at

rainbowmagicbooks.co.uk

You'll find activities, stories, a special newsletter
AND you can search for the fairy with your name!